D0231107

For Alan, with love

Bloomsbury Publishing,
London, Oxford, New York, New Delhi and Sydney

First published in Great Britain in 2015
by Bloomsbury Publishing Plc
50 Bedford Square, London, WC1B 3DP

Text and illustrations copyright © Emily MacKenzie 2015
The moral right of the author/illustrator has been asserted

All rights reserved
No part of this publication may be reproduced
or transmitted by any means,
electronic, mechanical, photocopying or otherwise,
without the prior permission of the publisher

A CIP catalogue record for this book
is available from the British Library

ISBN 978 1 4088 4312 3 (HB)
ISBN 978 1 4088 4313 0 (PB)
ISBN 978 1 4088 4311 6 (eBook)

Printed in China by Leo Paper Products, Heshan, Guangdong

5 7 9 10 8 6

All papers used by Bloomsbury Publishing are natural, recyclable products
made from wood grown in well-managed forests. The manufacturing processes
conform to the environmental regulations of the country of origin

www.bloomsbury.com

BLOOMSBURY is a registered trademark
of Bloomsbury Publishing Plc

WANTED!

Ralfy Rabbit, Book Burglar

by Emily MacKenzie

BLOOMSBURY

LONDON OXFORD NEW YORK NEW DELHI SYDNEY

Some rabbits dreamed
of lettuces and carrots.

Others dreamed of flowering
meadows and juicy dandelions.

But Ralfy
was a
little bit
different...

Ralfy dreamed about **books**.
In fact, he didn't just **dream** about them . . .
he wanted to read **all** the time.

Books I must read soon

Muddy Mysteries

The 39 Lettuces

Foxy Favourites

The Rabbit with the Dandelion Tattoo

Drama and Dragons

A Hutch with a View

Wild Adventures

The Railway Rabbits

Bunnivers Travels

Books to tell Mum about

Wuthering Carrots

A Tale of Two Warrens

Books Dad might like

Gone with the Carrots

THE GOOD, THE BAD AND THE BUNNY

One Flew over the Rabbit Hutch

Books to tell Tom and Betty about

The Rabbit, The Fox and The Wardrobe

The Waterbunnies

He made lists of all the books he had read (and gave them carrot ratings).
He made lists of all the books he **wanted** to read
(and placed them in category order).
He even made lists of books to recommend to his family and friends.

Monkey EEEEEK! ME HEARTIES! YIKES!
LANDLUBBER RAINFORES

OOOH
AAAAH

Ralfy **loved** to learn new words.
He **loved** the smell of books
and the **sound** of the **pages** flicking.

He **loved** getting lost in stories, pretending he was the
captain of a **pirate ship** or an intrepid **jungle explorer!**

AHOY
THERE

STRIPES

Swashbuckling CANOPY

Pieces of eight

FOLIAGE PARROT

Tige

JOLLY RO

AHOY

PROWL

SQUAWK!

I ♥ BOOKS

Yes,
Ralfy
LOVED
books . . .

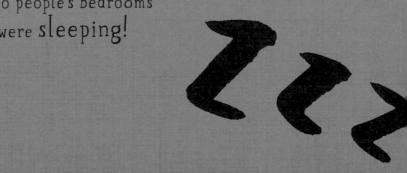

so much that he started **creeping** into people's bedrooms
and reading their books while they were **sleeping!**

And then one thing led to another.

Ralfy didn't just **read** the books, he **took** them home!

He crept off with comics and cookbooks,
dashed away with dictionaries,
nabbed novels and pinched poetry.

Ralfy had more books to read than **ever** before,
and he was **very** pleased with himself.

Arthur **loved** reading too.
He had shelves **buckling** with fairy tales, and bookcases
bursting with picture books. So when **gaps** started to appear
(along with half-eaten carrots and soggy lettuce leaves) and his **favourite** book
THE BIGGEST BOOK OF MONSTERS EVER
went **missing**, Arthur noticed.

ANIMAL STORIES

CLASSICS

ACTIVITY BOOKS

SOMEONE

was taking Arthur's books!

MONSTER BOOKS

SPACE ADVENTURES

SCARY STORIES

A super flashy torch

It was time to find out WHO!

Arthur assembled his special surveillance kit.
Then, with Teddy to keep him company,
he sat in the dark and waited . . . and waited.

BOOKS ON
STRING

SNAPPY
CAMERA

Teddy

Snacks

Notebook
and pencils

Binoculars

Chalk

STICKY
TAPE

Soon he heard a **rustle**. Arthur frantically
rummaged for his camera and his binoculars.
He shone his torch into the dark corners
of his room — and **that's** when he spotted Ralfy!

"STOP!
Come back here,
you little bunny
book thief,"
Arthur cried.

But it was **too late!**

Arthur was **furious!**

He told his mum, but she just laughed.
"A bunny book thief?
Arthur, I think your imagination is running wild."

He told his teacher, but she just said,
"Arthur, I want you to go away and have a long,
hard think about what you are saying."

THE BIGGEST BOOK of MONSTERS EVER

What could Arthur do?

That rascally rabbit had taken his favourite book of all time and **no one** believed him!

There was only **one** thing for it . . .

'ELLO, 'ELLO, 'ELLO!

Arthur called his local police station.

"A bunny book thief, you say. Well, fancy that!
Was there, ahem, anything unusual about
this rabbit? Can you give me a description?"
said PC Puddle, sniggering.

POLICE
STATION
HOTLINE

HA HA!

"Well, he was brown," said Arthur.
"With a fluffy white tail.
Oh, and he was wearing a T-shirt that said
I LOVE BOOKS."

With that, PC Puddle laughed out loud.
"I'll let you know if we discover anything," he snorted.

HA! HA! HA! HA! HA HA H

That night, Arthur felt **fed up**.

He went to bed **without** a story,
and he hardly slept at all.

Meanwhile, Ralfy had found **another**
house with plenty of books to pinch . . .

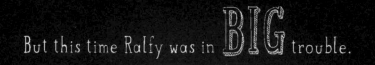

But this time Ralfy was in BIG trouble.

CAUGHT
IN THE ACT
BY A. POLICEMAN

He had burrowed up into PC Puddle's house!
"Well, well, well, what have we 'ere?" said PC Puddle.
"Could it be a little bunny book thief? Arthur was right all along!"

PC Puddle called Arthur straight away and told him he had caught the culprit *read*-handed! "Please come to the police station first thing tomorrow to identify your bunny book thief!" he said.

Easy! thought Arthur. There can't be many rabbits who wear I LOVE BOOKS T-shirts!

But he was **wrong**. Arthur had never seen **so** many rabbits –
and they were all wearing them!
This was going to be harder than he thought.

But then, PC Puddle pressed a big red button. An alarm bell rang and . . .

a conveyor belt of **goodies** started moving in front of
the bunny line-up. As lettuce leaves, carrots, apples and dandelions
whizzed by, all the rabbits began to feast — except for **one**.

CON-VEGGIE-BELT

Ralfy just wasn't interested . . .

until a very **special** treat passed by . . .

Ralfy couldn't resist!
In a frenzy, he started flicking
through a pile of books.

"Aha! Gotcha!"
said PC Puddle.
"You are in
BIG trouble!"

"I'm s-s-s-sorry!" stammered Ralfy.
"I just c-c-c-can't get enough books!"

"You mustn't just go
around stealing them,"
said PC Puddle. "You'll
have to put them all back!"

Suddenly Arthur began to feel sorry for Ralfy. After all, it was only because he **loved** books so much that he had managed to get himself into trouble.

"If you want lots and lots of books to **borrow**," said Arthur, "I know **exactly** where you can get them . . ."

Ralfy and Arthur are best 'book buddies' now
and love reading together whenever they can.
And they (especially Ralfy) **always** take the books back.

The library is their favourite place!

Note to reader: the next time you pop into your local library, be on the look out –
you might, just might, spot Ralfy and Arthur reading there too!